CORDUROY TAKES A BOW

OTHER BOOKS ABOUT CORDUROY

CORDUROY TAKES A BOW

Story by Viola Davis with B. G. Hennessy
Pictures by Jody Wheeler
Based on the characters created by Don Freeman

VIKING

VIKING

An imprint of Penguin Random House LLC

375 Hudson Street

New York, New York 10014

First published in the United States of America by Viking, an imprint of Penguin Random House LLC, 2018

A bear's share of the author's royalties from the sale of *Corduroy Takes a Bow* goes to the Lydia Freeman Charitable Foundation to support psychological care and research concerning children with disabilities, severe illnesses, or trauma.

LIBRARY OF CONGRESS CATALOGING-IN-PUBLICATION DATA IS AVAILABLE

ISBN 9780425291474

Printed in the U.S.A.

1   3   5   7   9   10   8   6   4   2

The art for this book was created using scratchboard and colored inks.

Jody Wheeler would like to acknowledge the BARC Youth Theatre Company in Ballston Spa, New York. Under the direction of Mike Gatzendorfer, children in grades 4 through 12 and their enthusiastic audiences enjoy the magic of live theater every summer.

*Genesis, you will always
be in the story! Love, Mom* —VD

To Clara —JHW

**To Don, creator of Corduroy
and a great lover of the theater** —The Freeman Foundation

It was just starting to snow when Lisa and her mother got off the bus in front of the theater. Lisa held Corduroy tight as they walked up the steps.

She had never been to a big theater like this before.
Neither had Corduroy. They had come to see
a performance of Mother Goose rhymes.

In the lobby, people were picking up tickets. Ushers handed out programs.
A brass chandelier hung from the ceiling that was painted with clouds.

Suddenly the lights flickered on and off. "That means the play will start
in a few minutes. We should find our seats," said Lisa's mother. Lisa held
her mother's hand a little tighter and held Corduroy a little closer.

The usher took their tickets and showed them where to sit.
"The seats are so soft!" said Lisa. She put Corduroy on her lap
and looked through the program.

Right before the play started, a very tall man sat down in front of Lisa.
"Mommy," Lisa whispered to her mother. "I can't see!"
"Here, dear," said her mother. "We can fold our coats together and
you can sit on top of them."

When Lisa stood up to sit on the coats, the orchestra started to play. She forgot all about Corduroy. He slipped off her lap and fell underneath the seats in front of them.

"Now *I* can't see anything," said Corduroy. "Maybe if I got closer to the music I could see the stage." He peeked down the aisle and saw some stairs.

When Corduroy got to the top step, the big red curtain went up, and up, and up. Corduroy was so startled that he lost his balance and tumbled into the orchestra pit. He looked around at all the musicians and thought, "This is a good spot to hear the music, but now I can't see the stage at all!"

At the back of the orchestra there was a tall set of drums. "Maybe if I sat up there I would have a better view," he thought. Quietly, he crawled through the orchestra, past feet, between instrument cases, and around music stands toward the drums.

"How did you get here, little fellow?" the drummer whispered to Corduroy. "You must be a prop from the play. Someone will be looking for you." He put Corduroy up on the ledge behind the drums.

There was a chair off to one side behind the curtain. "I could see better from there," thought Corduroy. But before he got to the chair, a stagehand tripped on him. "Sorry, bear!" said the stagehand. He put Corduroy on the table with the other props. The table was hard, not like Lisa's soft seat in the theater.

Backstage was very busy. Actors were coming and going, changing costumes and getting their props. One actor almost grabbed Corduroy!

"I should find a safer spot," he decided, and he hid between the costumes. "This is safe," he thought. "But I'll never see anything from here!"

There was a tree with a basket in its branches in the wing, off to one
side of the stage. "I would be able to see from there," Corduroy thought,
and he climbed up the tree and into the basket.

"Well," thought Corduroy, "this is more like it. Not too high, not too low. This is just right." He settled in and watched the Mother Goose performance. "I love the theater!" said Corduroy.

After a number of different scenes, the stage manager called out, "Final scene, everyone. Take your places!" Stagehands quickly moved new scenery onto the stage while the actors went to stand in position.

Suddenly, Corduroy's tree began moving right onto the stage.
Then it started to grow. Up, up, up went the tree, the basket,
and Corduroy!

"This is a very tall tree," said Corduroy as he looked down at the stage far below. The tall tree made him think of the tall man who sat in front of Lisa. Corduroy wondered, "How will I get back to Lisa if I'm up in this tree?"

On the stage below, Mother Goose started to sing,

Rock-a-bye baby
On the tree top,
When the wind blows
The cradle will rock.

Offstage, a fan blew air into the branches of the tree. The cradle
began to rock, back and forth, up and down, back and forth
and up and down. Corduroy was getting dizzy. He held on to
the sides of the cradle as it rocked faster and faster.

Mother Goose kept singing,

When the bough breaks
The cradle will fall.

And CRACK, the bough did break!

And down will come baby
Cradle and all.

Down, down, down came Corduroy. Cradle and all.

Before Corduroy knew what was happening, Mother Goose scooped him up for the curtain call.

The audience clapped as the actors bowed. Corduroy bowed, too.

After the curtain call, the cast took Corduroy backstage to the dressing room. "Who does this bear belong to?" they wondered.

The usher brought Lisa backstage.

"Corduroy, there you are!" said Lisa. "How did you get onstage?"

"I couldn't see, and I wanted to get a little closer," said Corduroy.

"Oh, Corduroy," said Lisa, "you certainly got closer!"

The very next day Lisa made a theater just for Corduroy.

He could see everything from a nice, safe spot.